P9-DHP-190

The Mystery at Misty Falls

by Kal Gezi and Ann Bradford
illustrated by Mina Gow McLean

THE CHILD'S WORLD

ELGIN, ILLINOIS 60120

Distributed by Childrens Press, 1224 West Van Buren Street, Chicago, Illinois 60607.

Library of Congress Cataloging in Publication Data

Gezi, Kalil I
  The mystery at Misty Falls.

  (The Maple Street five)
  SUMMARY: While at summer camp the five children from Maple Street solve the mystery of disappearing jewelry.
  [1. Camping—Fiction.   2. Raccoons—Fiction.
3. Mystery and detectives stories]   I. Bradford, Ann, joint author.   II. McLean, Mina Gow.   III. Title.
PZ7.G33902Mt   [E]   80-15708
ISBN 0-89565-147-5

Linda,

Barry,

Tom,

Maria,

and Vern . . .

were at summer camp. Many of the other children had already been there for two weeks. But this was the first day for the five children from Maple Street. The camp was named Misty Falls, after a high waterfall close by. Just now the children had gone for a walk to see the waterfall.

"Look!" Maria called. "A rainbow!" Sure enough, there in the mist of the waterfall was a brilliant rainbow.

"I never saw anything like that before!" said Tom. "Never!"

They watched the waterfall and the rainbow in awe.

The big bell rang, calling them back for supper. As they walked through the camp, they saw Jim, the grounds keeper.

Already, Jim was one of their favorite people. He had such good stories to tell! He told about the old times, when prospectors searched for gold along the river. Why, he'd even shown them a real gold nugget! It was his good-luck piece.

"Jim!" Barry called. But Jim just frowned and walked the other way.

"What's wrong with him?" Barry asked, puzzled.

"Who knows?" said Linda. "People are strange sometimes. My granddad gets like that."

"No, something's really wrong!" Barry said. But it was suppertime, and they had to hurry.

That night, all the campers gathered around the fire. The camp counselors, Julie and Nathan, came and talked to the five children. Both were college students. The kids liked them very much. Then the camp director talked. He told the group about the history of the camp.

As he was talking, Maria leaned over. "Look!" she whispered to Linda. Linda looked where she was pointing. There, on a table near the kitchen, was a large raccoon. Just then, the director saw the raccoon too.

"We have a visitor," he said softly. "Be very quiet. Don't scare him away."

All the campers watched as the raccoon picked up scraps of food from a plate.

"The cook always puts out scraps for him," said the director. "Raccoons are very smart, you know. But don't try to get too close to this one. He's not tame."

After the meeting, everyone was sleepy. Vern, Tom, and Barry headed for their cabin. Linda and Maria and another girl, Anne, had another cabin. Soon everyone in camp was sound asleep.

The next morning, Barry couldn't find his watch. "I know I put it right here!" he said. "Right on this shelf! Under this window!" But it wasn't there. Barry and Tom and Vern looked and looked, all over the cabin.

Finally, they had to stop. The breakfast bell was ringing.

After breakfast, the three boys came back to their cabin. There was Jim, just closing their door.

"Jim!" Barry called. Jim looked around quickly. "Why were you in our cabin?" Barry asked.

"Just fixing a loose board in the floor," Jim said. He turned to walk away.

"Did you see my watch while you were working?" Barry asked. "Under the bed or anywhere? It's missing. We looked all over for it."

At this Jim turned around and came back. "Your watch is missing?" he asked.

"Yes. Just since last night!"

"Well, then, I guess I should tell you that other things are missing."

"Other things?"

"Yes. Many campers have missed things. Julie lost her ring. Yesterday, my gold nugget disappeared."

"Is that what was wrong with you yesterday?" asked Barry.

Jim nodded. "I was really upset. That nugget is worth a lot of money."

Later that day, the five children discussed the thefts. "Let's ask Julie about her missing ring," Maria said. "Maybe she will remember a clue or something."

But Julie wasn't much help. "It was just gone," she said. "I left it on the shelf in my cabin when I went to take a shower. When I got back, the ring was gone. That's all I know."

Camp life went on as usual. There was swimming every day. There were all kinds of nature classes. Maria took Nathan's birdwatching class. Tom took a tracking class. The other children took the swimming class.

More and more things turned up missing. People were getting angry and suspicious.

"I sure wish we could find out who the thief is," said Maria one day. "I don't like not trusting people."

One afternoon, Maria saw Nathan heading away from camp. She ran to catch up with him.

"Hey, Nathan!" she called. "Are you going bird watching?"

"Huh? Oh . . . uh . . . yeah."

"Can I go too?"

"Uh . . . not today. This is a solo trip. My day off, you know."

"Oh. Well, see you."

"Sure."

Maria walked back, thinking. "Nathan had a shovel with him," she told the others. "Why would he take a shovel if he's going bird watching?"

"Maybe he's not going bird watching," said Barry. "Maybe he's the thief. Maybe he buried all the stolen stuff and is going to dig it up."

"No, I don't think so," said Maria. "Not Nathan."

"Could be," said Linda.

"Well," said Vern. "I don't think we should say that unless we have proof."

Soon it was time for the treasure hunt. Julie told the children to look for a red treasure box. Barry, Tom, Maria, Linda, and Vern went together. They walked down the path leading to the river. There was no sign of any red treasure box. Soon they heard the sound of someone digging.

"Look there!" Barry whispered.

It was Nathan, digging hard. The children ran toward him.

"What are you doing?" Tom asked.

"Well," Nathan said. "I guess it won't hurt if you know. I've been searching for gold since we came here. But I haven't found any."

Nathan told them he was worried. College was costing so much! He didn't know whether he would have enough money to finish.

"See," said Vern. "I told you not to be too suspicious. All he's doing is searching for gold."

The children returned to camp. Anne greeted them. She had found the hidden treasure. A dollar bill was inside the box!

Very early the next morning, the big bell clanged. It clanged and clanged and clanged. Soon everyone was running to see what was wrong.

"The kitchen is a mess!" said the camp director. "Someone seems to think it's funny to scatter flour everywhere. But it isn't funny at all!"

The campers crowded around to look in the kitchen. The cook stomped back and forth, very angry! Flour covered everything. Broken eggs and overturned jelly added to the mess.

"Look!" Tom called. "I think I know who did it!" He pointed to some tracks in the flour. "Raccoon tracks!" he said.

"But how?" asked the cook. "I always lock the door!"

"Do you lock the windows too?" asked Jim. "Raccoons can climb, you know. And they can unlock latches."

"Never thought of that," said the cook. He looked around. "That raccoon!" he said. "That's the last time I feed him!" He shook his head. Then he began to laugh. He laughed and laughed and laughed. Soon everyone else was laughing too, even the camp director.

The campers pitched in and helped the cook clean up the mess. And camp life settled back to normal.

"Well," said Linda, "that mystery was easy enough to solve. Wish we could solve the mystery of who is stealing everyone's jewelry." But no one had a clue.

That night, as the campers sat around the fire, the raccoon visited again. But he found no food. The cook was still angry at him. So, after searching the table top, he ambled off into the darkness.

"I wonder . . . ," said Tom. "If that raccoon can get in one window. . . ." Tom motioned to the others to follow him. And he set off to see where the raccoon was going.

Through the woods, the five children walked. They tried to keep the raccoon in sight. Once or twice, they lost the raccoon in the darkness. But the raccoon was in no hurry. So they always managed to find him again. Finally, the raccoon climbed into an old, dead tree trunk.

In a minute, he climbed out again and moved away.

"Let's check out that tree trunk," said Tom. The children flashed their flashlights into the opening. Something sparkly caught the light.

"Look!" yelled Linda. It was Jim's gold nugget.

"And there's my watch!" said Barry.

"And look at this ring! It must be Julie's."

The children gathered up all the bright, sparkly objects and carried them back to camp.

"Hey, where have you been?" asked Julie when she saw them. "We were beginning to worry about you."

"We found the thief and all the things he stole!" said Tom. "It was the raccoon! All this stuff was in his den! He must like shiny things!"

Soon all the lost items were returned. Jim smiled broadly when the children gave him his nugget. "Sure glad to see that!" he said. "Got special plans for this nugget!"

The next day was the last day at camp for the Maple Street five. Jim helped them pack. They lugged their duffel bags out to the bus. Just then, Nathan came running out of the woods.

"Look!" he called. "Look what I found! A piece of gold! You were right, Jim! That hill was the place to look!"

"Ohh!" said Maria. "Let me see!"

She looked at the nugget in Nathan's hand. It was Jim's nugget. "Why," she said, "that looks like . . ."

"Like a mighty fine piece of gold!" Jim interrupted. He winked at Maria, who still stood there with her mouth open.

"Yes," said Maria. "Like a mighty fine piece of gold."

Nathan hurried off to show Julie his gold.

"You won't tell him it's mine, will you?" Jim said. "I don't want him to know."

"It's the secret of Misty Falls," said Vern. "And you can bet we'll keep it!"

The children all said their good-byes. They hugged Jim and promised to write to him.

As the bus moved up the road, the children looked back. From the high mountain, Misty Falls cascaded down to the valley. Suddenly, a rainbow formed in its mist.

"This," said Tom, "is one place I'll never forget!"